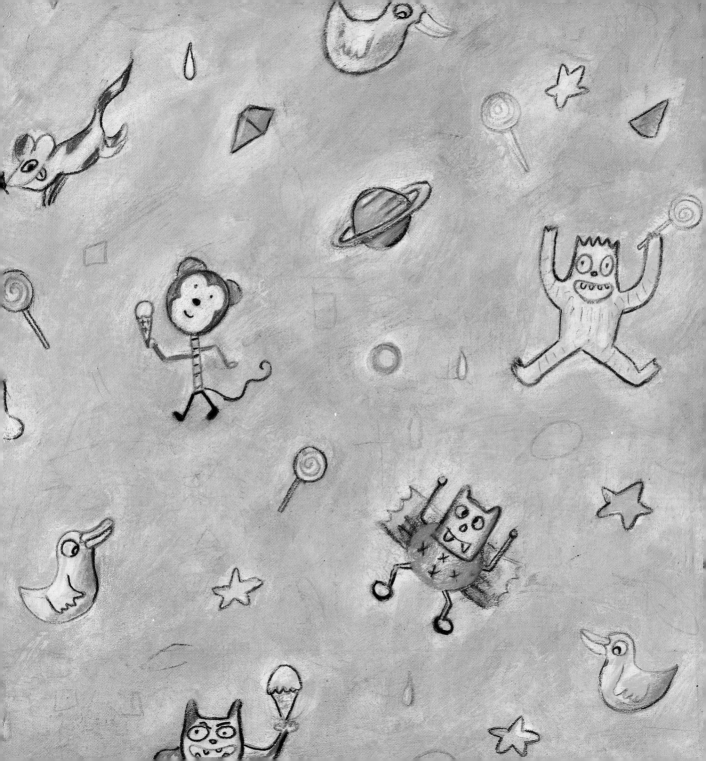

MOMMY DOESN'T KNOW MY NAME

MOMMY DOESN'T KNOW MY NAME

Suzanne Williams

Illustrated by Andrew Shachat

Houghton Mifflin Company   Boston

For Ward and Emily, my children, and for
Mildred "Billie" Hannah, my grandmother
— S. W.

For Lisa and Hollis, Grandma Ruth, and all
my new friends in Santa Cruz — A. S.

Text copyright © 1990 by Suzanne Williams
Illustrations copyright © 1990 by Andrew Shachat

Manufactured in the China
SCP 20 19 18 17 16 15 14 13 12 11

Library of Congress Cataloging-in-Publication Data

Williams, Suzanne.
  Mommy doesn't know my name / Suzanne Williams: illustrated by
Andrew Shachat.
    p.   cm.
    Summary: Mommy calls Hannah all sorts of names except her own,
leaving Hannah to wonder if Mommy really does know who she is.
    ISBN 0-395-54228-6   PAP ISBN 0-395-77979-0
    [1. Names, Personal—Fiction. 2. Identity—Fiction. 3. Mothers
and daughters—Fiction.] I. Shachat, Andrew, ill. II. Title.
PZ7.W66824Mo   1990   89-78205
[E]—dc20   CIP   AC

Mommy doesn't know my name.

When I wake up in the morning
she comes in to get me.
"Is that my little chickadee?" she says.

I'm not a chickadee.

I'm Hannah.

After I'm dressed we have breakfast.
My cup slips, and I spill orange juice.
"Oh, no," I cry.

"It's O.K., pumpkin," says Mommy.
"Accidents happen to everyone."
Do accidents happen to pumpkins?

I'm not a pumpkin. I'm Hannah.

Soon we are at Sharon's house.

Mommy gives me a kiss.

"See you later, alligator," she says.

I'm not an alligator!
I'm Hannah.

When we are home again Mommy makes dinner.

I'm hungry and can't wait.

"You little devil," says Mommy.

"Go wash your hands."

I'm not a devil. I'm Hannah.

After dinner we do a puzzle.

Then Mommy reads her book.

I want to play some more.

"Boo!" I shout.

"Help!" screams Mommy. "It's a monster."

I'm not a monster. I'm Hannah.

Mommy puts on some music and we dance.

Around and around we twirl.

Mommy gets tired and has to sit down.

I keep dancing.

I make silly faces and kick my feet in the air.

"You funny monkey," says Mommy.
She laughs.

I'm not a monkey. I'm Hannah.

When it is bedtime we have a story.
Mommy sings a good-night song,
but I want to talk some more.
"Shh," says Mommy.
"Be a quiet little mouse."

I sit up in my bed.
"I'm not a mouse," I say,
"I'm Hannah!"

"Yes, I know," says Mommy.
She gives me a hug.
"You're Hannah.
My very own happy little, funny little girl."

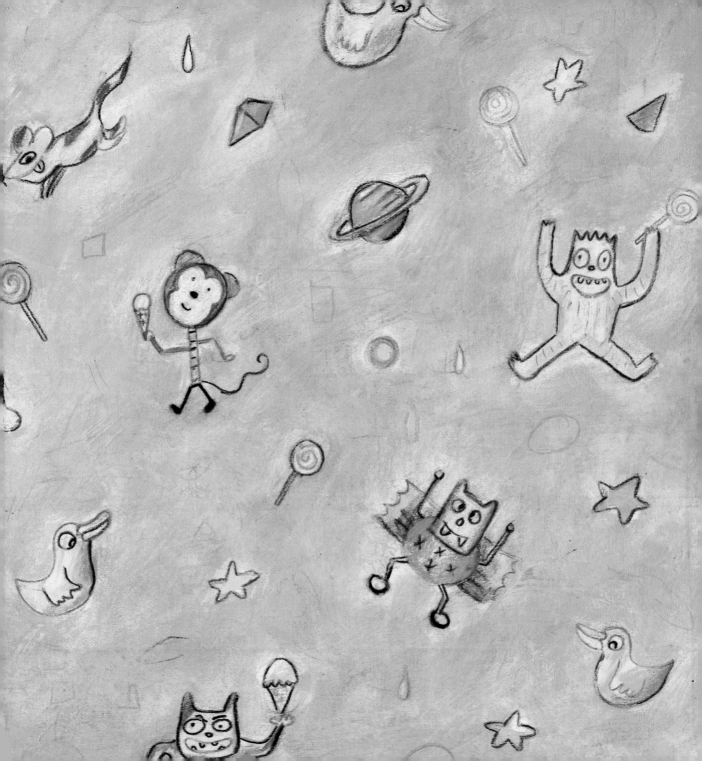